THE REALM OF FIRE

DAN ABSALONSON

The Realm of Fire

Visit the author's website:
www.DanDanTheArtMan.com

Give feedback on the book at
danabso@gmail.com

First Edition
Printed in the U.S.A.

DEDICATION

This book is dedicated to my daughter McKenzie. She shares my love of reading, and also really enjoys the fantasy genre. I think she will like this story. It has been a joy to see her become a voracious reader. I'm glad I helped her decide how to spend her money when she had saved up a considerable amount. I told her about eReaders and she was all about it. I helped her purchase one and the rest was history. She uses it well, reading countless books as her device rearranges its tiny ink granules onto her digital screen. I'm so happy to have shared the gift of reading fiction with her and I hope this book inspires more readers to get out there and find their next great adventure in the pages of a book whether that be on paper or a screen!

PART ONE

I knew I was in trouble when my father's men found me hiding in a tree next to the army practice field.

"You must come down at once Prince Drefan. You are needed in the…"

"Yes I know I am supposed to be at my lesson."

"No your Highness. You are needed elsewhere. We cannot speak on it here. Please hurry Sire."

"Of course," I said dropping down. As

I followed them I noticed for the first time that it was much colder than usual for that time of year. They lead me to the wizards living quarters, a place I seldom visited. As we entered I saw my father King Eadric, and brother Prince Aethelfrith, standing next to Wizard Nerian's bed. He lay there looking more haggard and thin than I had ever seen him. I realized I had not seen the dear wizard in many days. I walked up to the bed and stood beside my father.

"Fool boy. Sneaking off like that," my father said.

"I was just…"

"Silence. We have little time and we already wasted some finding you. Listen now. Please tell him Nerian."

I turned to the wizard.

"Tell me what?"

He brushed down the part of his white beard that lay below his lips and spoke.

"I am dying my Prince and there is no

one to replace me as wizard. The kingdom needs you and you must leave soon."

"Where must I go? Tell me and I will leave at once. Why have you not already sent a messenger Father? Surely there is a rider more skilled than I..."

"Just listen to him Son," Father said spitting out his words while trying to hold back his temper.

The wizard opened his mouth to speak but began coughing instead. He held up his hand. His bone thin fingers looked like the gnarled branches of a tree, his veins twisting up like roots searching for water. His hacking subsided and he spoke in a feeble voice I had never heard from him before.

"My power is fading. Soon I will pass on, and the kingdom will need a wizard. You my Prince are the only one who can become one."

"A wizard? You have the wrong man

Nerian. I am to be a soldier, I cannot..."

"Silence boy. Listen to him," my father barked.

Being a wizard was the last thing I wanted to do. I wanted to lead our army into battle someday with a sword in my hand, not a wizard's staff.

"You must replace me Prince Drefan. My power is leaving me. The kingdom grows colder every day. There will come a time when I can no longer hold back the great storms of the West that consume everything. Our people will not survive, and only one with royal blood can travel to the Realm of Fire. Your kingdom needs you your Highness. I am as surprised as you my prince. I thought that I still had many lifetimes to live before I had to pass on my position and knowledge. You must listen to me."

I looked at my father thinking that surely it was all a mistake. The implications of what he was saying hit me hard. He was a royal, a prince like me. Nerian spoke again.

"It is said dragons come from the Realm of Fire, though none know how to get there. It is said to be a land wholly different from our own. There is no road that will take you there, no great body of water on which you can sail to its shores. Legend says the only way to get there is through fire."

"Yes and who in the burnt realm knows what that means?"

"I know what it means dear boy, and I am the only one in the kingdom who does. I have been there. It is from that realm that my power comes and where yours will come as well."

I almost spoke to protest again, but heeded my father's warning.

"Look upon my staff."

I picked up his staff which was resting

against his bed. It was much lighter than I had expected. On the end was affixed a long claw of some kind. It was dark red in color. It looked like it had turned that way from age but I had always known it to be the brightest of reds. It always stood out among the drab colors of Nerian's robes.

"What you are holding young prince is…"

"Your fire staff," I said in a whisper.

"Yes. On the top rests the cleaved talon of a great dragon I once faced in my youth as you must face now."

My mind went from curiosity to terror. I felt my heart thump faster in my chest. I looked at the talon on the staff with a new sense of wonder and respect for the old wizard.

"The dragon's talon is the source of power. It has always been bright, but as you can see its power is now fading. It has lasted me many lifetimes, keeping my body and this kingdom safe, but soon I will pass on and join my friends who have died and left me behind over the years."

The wizard's speech was broken up once again by hacking coughs.

"The orb of finding leads you to sources of magic. There is a tall tree in the middle of the Red Forest. You must get far away from the magic of my staff for the orb to point toward the tree. Travel East and let the sands of fire in its spherical body guide you to the portal tree. You will need an axe as well, when you get to the portal tree you will see high upon its trunk a great symbol carved into the wood. With any luck it should still bear a red glow though I fear it may have nearly faded. Splash some potion from my study I labeled tree kill onto the base of the tree. It will only take a few good blows with a sharp axe to cut the tree down, then cut around the symbol. Take some charcoal and parchment with you to copy the symbol. Be precise my Prince, it must be just as you see it carved into the tree. Once that is done build a great fire then cast the piece of wood with the symbol upon it into the flames. This will create a portal to the Realm of Fire."

The wizard stopped, waving his hand toward the glass of water beside his bed. My brother walked over and gave it to him. He took a slow shallow drink and then gave it back.

"Thank you."

The wizard looked to me again.

"Once you see the fire cloaked in a bright red blanket of power, step into it, you will not be burned. Let us hope there is still enough power left in the symbol I carved upon the tree ages ago to send you through. Once there you must find a dragon. The bigger they are the more power they hold. Wait until it slumbers and then sneak upon his den."

The wizard stopped talking to cough something up. He leaned over and spit upon the stone floor then lay back down and continued.

"It must be a male dragon. They have horns while females do not. You will need to chop off the talon from its longest finger then you will need to run for safety. You must leave the realm immediately.

All the powers of the staff are written in a book I keep in my study. It is bound in a dark leather volume. When you return you will need to study it well so you can serve your kingdom with its power. Never let it fall into the hands of enemies. I do not have much time left. Soon the power of my staff will run out. The portal will die with me. Now go my Prince."

I wanted to laugh, or cry, or say something to convince them all that this was insanity. Yes, I wanted to be a warrior someday but how could I face a dragon? A great beast whose kind I thought were long dead. They were from legends and fancy tales, not something you could actually go out and find. I could not get any words to come out. To my surprise my father spoke for me.

"I have known you all my life Nerian so I know you would not say these things unless they were of the most importance. Would it not be wise for my best men to go with him?" I do not wish my son to be put in such danger. The wizard held up a hand as he coughed into another. Once his coughs subsided he spoke.

"My Lord, I wish you could send your entire army with the boy, but the portal will only allow him through Sire. Only one with royal blood. That is how the ancients set it up so common men could not travel into the realm and capture this great power for themselves."

"Then I will go with him. Surely I can protect him." To my great surprise my brother spoke. It was the first time I learned he had love for me for he only showed me pain and embarrassment.

"I fear we cannot put the heir to the throne in such danger Your Majesty."

With tears in his eyes my father put his hand on Aethelfrith's shoulder.

"Nerian is right my son. We must keep you safe so the kingdom has someone to take my place when I pass on. We cannot risk it. There is no other heir and your brother is the only other who can journey through this portal our dear wizard speaks of."

My father straightened his robes and stood taller. He cleared his throat, tilted back his crown, and wiped away his tears.

"All those days sneaking off to see the soldiers train might come to your aid now my petulant boy."

He looked over at me with a sad but forceful grin on his face.

"Go now to Nerian's study and gather what you need. I will meet you in the stables with the finest axe the blacksmith has to offer, and it is high time I gave you your first sword."

I was barely listening to what my father was saying. It was all I could do to keep the panic from spilling out in hot messy tears. My breaths were heavy and my ears felt as though they were stuffed with cotton, but when my father said the word sword I came out of it.

"Wait, I finally get a sword? I will go on this journey and become a wizard as long as I get to keep the sword."

"Big surprise," my brother said.

"That is the son I know. May it bring you courage my boy. Now go!"

PART TWO

In the wizard's study, a dark and musty chamber, there were bound books and scrolls everywhere. I wondered, for the first time, if I would ever find a love for reading that he had. I doubted he had any tales of heroes going on adventures in his dusty tomes. I walked over to his desk where a great many books were piled next to his broad pipe.

Above the desks were shelves with more books. Between a set of dark blue and faded green book spines sat an orb upon a black blanket. I took it down from the shelf and gazed into it. Inside the glass was red sand. It clung to the side of the orb facing the wizard's bed chambers where his staff leaned against his bed. Some mysterious force was pulling the sand toward the nearest source of magic. It took a great effort to stop looking at the orb but I tore my eyes away from it, took one final look around the study wondering if I would ever return to it and claim it as my own, then set off toward the stables.

My father was there with my brother. A strong horse named Fristle, who was white with brown spots, was saddled up with a bedroll and pack strapped to his back.

My father was holding a handsome sword that looked small in his hands.

"Here my boy," he said handing it to me.

The blacksmith said it will do well in your hands. It was made with a reduced length, but hold it out."

I did, swinging it around the way I saw the soldiers do it when I spied on them from my tree.

"Yes that sword fits you well. I see you do not have trouble handling its weight. That is good."

I held it up and turned it over. It was the most beautiful thing I had ever seen, and it was mine.

"Thank you Father. I will cherish this blade."

My father laughed.

"I know you will. Now put this sheath on and put it away before you run off to court the thing."

My brother laughed, but it was not his usual cruel laugh. I looked over at him. He held an axe for me. I put the sheath on my back and slid the sword where it belonged. I looked up and my eyes met with my brother's.

"It looks good on you," he said.

I had never seen the sincere look that was upon his face in that moment.

"Please come back to us. I know I give you nothing but trouble and bruises, but you are my brother and I love you. Return home safely to us. Use that sword well. Be the hero you have always dreamed of being, and come back so that someday we can rule this land together. I wish I could go with you and protect you, but this is your quest. May this axe fell the great tree swiftly for you. Be careful, it has been sharpened well. I love you Brother."

He handed the axe to me. I was surprised to see him acting this way, but it also warmed my heart to see that he truly cared for me. It just took a journey likely ending in my death for him to tell me.

"Thank you Aethelfrith. I love you too Brother."

"Make me proud son, and please come back to us. Your mother needs you. I and your brother need you. Most of all your kingdom needs you. Return with power from the dragons and help us rule over this land with the protection of your magic for another age. We are all counting on you son."

He grabbed my brother and pulled him in close.

"Make us proud."

The tears were in his eyes again. He pulled me in and we embraced. Then he let go of my brother and I and took me by the shoulders. He looked me up and down.

My father drew us both in again and then waved his hand toward my horse. I climbed up into the saddle and looked down at them.

"There is some food in your pack, warm blankets, and the parchment and charcoal you will need. Stay safe my son. Return to us."

"I will," I heard the words come out of my mouth more than spoke them. I tried not to think about the danger before me and bid them farewell. I rode out of the castle, through the gate of the outer battlements, and on to the East road.

I rode for a long time until I could tell Fristle was tired. I hopped off of him and lead him to a stream. While he drank I pulled the orb of finding out of my pack. The crimson sand inside was no longer pressing against the glass toward the castle. Now it was pointing me East toward the forest.

"We are getting closer Fristle!" I said.

He blew out some air in a dismissive way. I envied his ignorance of the danger that awaited us. I corrected thoughts realizing he would not be plunged into the fire realm, but I alone would face that danger. I put the orb away and unsheathed my sword. I hoped that looking at it would replace my growing fear with the joy of holding my own sword. It did feel amazing just pulling it from my back. It worked for a few seconds. It is such a beautiful blade, but I could not stop thinking about facing a dragon for long.

Once Fristle had rested and eaten his fill of the grass around us, we continued East. Soon the meager landscape of rolling hills was replaced by tall thick trees, and the wind blew stronger at the higher elevation. It made the branches of the trees look like great hairy arms beckoning me into the forest.

They swayed, sounding like a multitude of voices whispering secrets of the magic within. As we left the meadow the dark dense forest surrounded us swallowing up the comforting heat of the sun. I shivered in my saddle and focused my eyes trying to look for a trail as my vision adjusted to the shade. The trees gave off a strong fresh smell. I turned around and reached into my pack for the orb of finding.

As I held it before me the sand inside

looked much brighter than it had in the sunlight. It pushed toward the glass in one large clump, directing me further into the forest. I rode on at a slow pace, Fristle picking his way through tall foliage, massive rocks, and fallen trees. I kept my left hand on the saddle as my right held up the orb. The sand began to shift to the left. I turned Fristle until it once again clung to the glass directly away from us. We continued on like that for a long time.

As night began to fall, I hopped off of Fristle and let him rest and eat again, and we made our way further into the forest. Just when I thought I should stop to make camp, and continue our quest in the morning, I noticed the sand had become more violent. Each grain pressed past the others in waves against the glass trying to get closer to the magical source.

As we rode on, the sand began to glow ever so slightly. I might not have noticed if the forest had not been so dark, though the trees grew farther apart and our path was easier to traverse. I pushed my heels into Fristle's sides urging my tired horse to transition from a trot to a canter. I posted, standing in the saddle. My stomach and back were tired and my legs began to burn but I wanted to find that tree. As scared as I was, I wanted to see the magic symbol and the portal.

Then the sand shifted, racing back toward me. I stopped Fristle and looked up behind us. We had been moving fast and must have passed it. Turning around we walked back the way we had come. The only thing I could see up there were sparse patches of sunlight shooting through the branches. The sand in the orb was clumped up at the top of the glass. I looked up but did not see anything at first. Then I thought I saw the smallest glimmer of red. I got off of Fristle, walked up to the trunk of the tree, and looked up. There was a faint red glow a long way up through the branches. I walked over to Fristle and got my axe. Then I led him to a tree a few paces away, tied him to it, and got to work.

I took out Nerian's potion and splashed it across the tree. It ate away with an appetite spreading a rough cut through the wood. Smoke rose into the air like pungent curling locks of aged gray hair. It reminded me of Nerian's hair and I wondered if he was still alive. Once the smoke cleared I poured the remaining potion into the tree pushing the cut further in past the center. It went almost all the way through. The great tree teetered making loud cracking sounds. I hefted the axe. It took only four swings from the other side to send the tree crashing to the forest floor. I ran toward the top of the tree where the strange symbol was carved into the trunk. I wondered at the way its form glowed red from magic wielded upon it ages ago.

"Fristle these dragons must be powerful if one of their talons contains magic that lasts like this through the ages."

He snorted again as if to say he was the most powerful beast in all the land. I ran to him and got the parchment and charcoal from my pack. Then I ran to the symbol and began copying each line and curve with great care. My heavy fingers took more coaxing to move as they were sore from gripping Fristle and swinging the axe. It took me a while but that was okay, I did not want to find out what would happen if I had one of the markings off when I was on the other side of the portal trying to get back home.

With my work finished I looked back and forth from the glowing symbol to the parchment. For once I was thankful for my lessons. I rolled the parchment up and walked back to my horse securing it in my pack.

I got to work chopping wood until there was enough for a great fire. I cut around the symbol and placed it safely next to Fristle. I stacked log upon log until I had constructed an enormous cone of wood ready to burn. Beneath I slid many small pieces of wood and handfuls of dry grass. With my tinderbox I set the grass and wood aflame. First came smoke, then small flames, and after a time they reached high above my head like great dancing spirits.

The heat was more intense than I could have imagined. I picked up the big chunk of wood with the symbol on it, hoping the wizard was right, and threw it into the fire.

As I watched the flames flicker and sway, the heat of the fire diminished and a red glow began to encompass it. Not knowing how long I would be or if I would ever return I ran over to Fristle and untied his rope so he could return home. All the while I kept glancing at the fire hoping its red glow would stay strong. As soon as my horse was free I turned to the red glowing flames, screamed for courage, and ran.

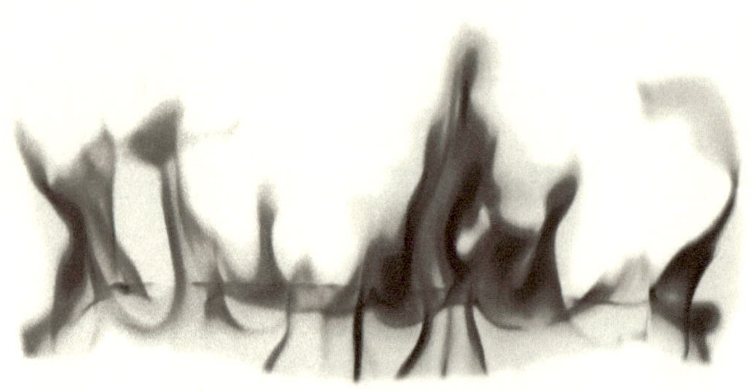

PART THREE

I ran toward the cold flame. It was big and bright and colder than the darkest night of winter. I shivered. My limbs felt numb. I kept running. The red consumed me. It was all. Nothing had ever been but the red glow. My eyes were shut tight but the red shined through. Then I felt warmth returning to my body and the bright light began to fade. I opened my eyes. I was in the Realm of Fire.

The air was still. The red and cold faded away, and then a great gust of air blew me onto my back. I heard what sounded like an enormous tent being erected, or perhaps a flag the size of our castle flapping in the wind. I sat up and looked to the heavens. It was a dragon. A massive red dragon with horns!

I looked around for shelter. I did not want to become supper for the beast. Behind me was a massive boulder. I got up and stumbled behind it. I waited until I could hear that he had flown well past me. I could tell he was not close to me anymore but when I poked my head around the rock I still expected him to dive for me, but he was a dark shape in the distance.

I looked around at the strange place I had been spit into. Everything was red. The rocks were gray, with a red hue. The leaves of the trees were maroon. The sky was like a big wash of crimson paint, sprinkled about with sprays of auburn rain clouds. Suddenly my lesson room back at the castle did not seem so gloomy. Yes, I finally had a sword, an axe, and a magic talisman, but it looked like I had been dropped into hades and now I had to find a dragon!

I started walking in the direction of the beast who had knocked me over with a gust from his powerful wings. I could still see his dark form flapping in the distance. He flew left toward a mountain that blocked him from my view.

Despite being more tired than I had ever been, I kept walking. I wondered how soldiers could march all day with weapons strapped to their bodies.

As I trudged on I started to lose hope of finding the dragon. He had passed out of my view and there was no way I could keep up with him. I kept my eyes to the sky in hopes of finding another one even though deep down I never wanted to see another one for as long as I lived. I crested a hill and the side of a great mountain came into view. I could see smoke coming from a huge cave which sat a long way up the mountain. It looked like someone had constructed a fire as big as my portal flame and that a giant was blowing its smoke out into the sky. A great plume of smoke floated out from the cave and then up into the air to join with the reddish clouds.

I continued on to the mountain, and began my ascent. After walking for a while it became too steep to stay on my legs. The axe and sword strapped to my back felt like great hands reaching up to pull me away from the mountain. I leaned forward and began to climb on my hands and knees. It was steep but there were plenty of trees and rocks which supplied me with secure hand and footholds. And I kept climbing.

Though I was sweating from the excursion I noticed it was getting colder the farther I climbed. I dared not turn and look down. The air felt thinner and the smell of something like rotten eggs was beginning to bother me. The higher I climbed, the stronger it became. Soon I felt like I was climbing up the cracked side of a massive egg, its spoiled yolk spilling into my nostrils with each deep and labored breath.

My arms and legs ached as I reached a ridge. I stopped and turned to see the view my progress up the mountain had afforded me. I was a long way up from where I started. The trees and rocks that had been my guide all seemed to be pointing away from me toward the base of the mountain like friends beckoning me to stop my deadly quest and climb back down to safety. To my right was the hill. The one that had blocked my view of the dragon, and taken me forever to walk over. From my new vantage point it looked like a tiny bump in the vast red landscape.

I held my breath to listen for the dragon. I could barely hear his breathing farther up the mountain, slow and even. I hoped he was asleep. The smell was much worse and I could feel heat coming from above me. I kept climbing.

It sounded like the dragon was an arm's reach away. I gripped a rock and pulled myself up to a flat area. In front of me was the cave and bright red patches of the dragon's scales. They were hard to see though because they were obscured by the smoke pouring out of his nostrils in great bursts with each exhalation. He was much bigger than I had imagined. Bigger, it seemed, than my mind or courage could handle. I lowered myself back down and turned my back to him.

There was no way I was going right up

to that thing and chopping one of his talons off without waking him and getting away alive. My body was shaking. I pulled out my sword and looked at it. I thought about what I had always dreamed of being. A brave warrior. Someone who faced the enemy and charged forward. I put my sword back, turned around, and started climbing.

I made it to the mouth of the cave, my body still shaking. I tried to make each footstep lighter than the last as I got closer to the great beast. I pulled out my axe knowing I would have to do it before I lost my courage or I would never be able to get it done. Nerian had said dragons were deep sleepers and he was knowledgeable in all things so with my last ounce of courage, I stopped trying to be quiet and ran.

I came into the dark cave. The smoke was thick and putrid. I kept running through the haze toward the red scales shifting up and down. I could see one of his hands stretched out on the ground just at the edge of the light pouring in from behind me.

I raised my axe not daring to look at the dragon's head. I thought one look could send me running back down the mountain or freeze me in fear. I came upon the massive hand. The fingers were the size of my legs and the talons curling out like daggers spanned the length of my forearm.

Just as Nerian had said above the talon the thick scales stopped and there was a thin ring of soft red dragon flesh. I brought the axe down with all my might. I struck it in the right spot and my axe did its work slicing through the tip of the dragon's finger and bouncing off the hard stone floor of the cave.

The dragon's head shot up. Its eyes and mouth opened then it let out a deafening howl that made me jump back.

I dropped the axe, urinated into my pants, grabbed the massive red talon and ran. I could feel the dragon's mighty body crawling toward me through the shaking ground. When I was close to the edge of the plateau I looked back and he was right behind me. I don't know what I was thinking, or why I did it, but I saw a tree branch and I jumped for it.

I flew over the steep slope of the mountain side and landed just above the tree branch I was aiming for as though the tree caught me. I tried to drop down but my pack was stuck in the branches. I got one arm out of a strap but the other was stuck tight. I panicked and pulled as hard as I could but it would not move. I reached up and unsheathed the sword. I slid it between my shoulder and the strap then pushed. My sword cut through and I fell past the branch I wanted to land on to a thinner one much farther below. Once again the tree caught me.

I felt a brilliant heat press down on me from above. I looked up and saw the tree and my pack on fire. I did not know what I was going to do but I still did not want to die so I scrambled down the tree as fast as I could. I made it back down to the blessed earth and looked for a hiding place. I did not want to go back down the mountain because I had to move fast and I was afraid I would trip and fall to my death. Instead, I headed across the steep incline. I looked up and saw the dragon circling back around to try and find me. I kept running.

PART FOUR

As I ran I spotted a thick patch of shrubbery. I dove into its mess of branches and let them pull in around me. I laid low to the ground, smelling the red earth up close for the first time. It smelled similar to the dirt of my world, but somehow redder like cinnamon. I remained still and listened.

It was easy to hear where the dragon was. His massive wings beat the air in enormous arcs, sending thunderous sounds my way. For a time he flew all around the mountain staying near to where I hid. Then he started flying farther down the mountain. I did not want to risk getting eaten or burned to death so I stayed hidden in the itchy arms of those thick bushes. After a lifetime I could hear his wings flapping no more. It was only then that I remembered the parchment with the symbol. I needed it to get home, but it had been inside my pack. That was turned into black ash, destroyed by the dragon's breath.

I sat up and raised myself to a crouch. My head popped above the top of the bushes. I looked around. I listened. The dragon was nowhere to be found. Somehow I had survived. I felt a sense of relief. With death no longer at hand my mind was able to think again and I came to a horrible realization. My pack and the symbol on the parchment were gone.

I might as well have been eaten or burned to death. Now I had no way of getting back to my family. To my home. I stood and leapt out of the bushes, brushing small broken pieces of it off of me. I collapsed to the dirt and cried until there was a tiny pool of mud beneath my face. I sat up, sniffed, wiped my nose, felt sorry for myself, and cried some more.

I was doomed to die in the desolate kingdom of red. The place of dragons, scorched earth, and crimson skies. The Realm of Fire.

I wanted to lie back down and die. I wished the dragon had killed me. At least then I would not have to starve to death wandering around in a blood red world that was devoid of all comfort; knowing that I failed everyone I loved and the kingdom I was born to protect.

I looked at the dragon's talon. It was longer than my middle finger and about half as wide as my wrist at its base. It was a deep shiny red color that seemed to pull your eyes toward it as you looked at it.

Still crying, I began tracing lines in the dirt with the talon. They glowed red for a moment; drying up the bit of mud from my tears, and then they were just lines in the sand. I stopped and looked at the talon and thought hard about what the symbol looked like.

I began drawing it in the dirt. The red glow clung to the ground with each line I drew and then slowly faded away. I kept working. When I could not remember what line came next I closed my eyes and pictured myself sitting on the tree with my back against the mountain holding the parchment. Then it would come to me. I kept working and finished the symbol.

The freshest red lines in the dirt were glowing, but disappeared moments later. The symbol was just dull lines drawn in the dirt. I studied it, giving it my full attention. My tutor would have been proud. It looked correct, but the magic left its mark and then vanished. I was about to wipe it away when I remembered there was one last line curving off the bottom right of the symbol. I put the talon to the ground and drew the line with all the precision I could render from my tired hands.

A strong red glow much brighter than Nerian's symbol in the tree shone with such brilliance I wiped it away fearing it would draw the attention of the dragon. I stood up and made my way back up to his cave. When he returned I would be ready for him and his deadly burning breath would bring me home.

The smell in the cave was still strong and fowl but I stuck to my purpose. This was my only way home. I turned around and ran to the ledge then jumped to the tree where my pack once hung. I landed on the tree. Dark burnt bark was above and below me but the tree was still strong enough to hold me. I held the talon tight and began to carve into the blackened wood.

As I did, it spread intense red lines. As I formed the symbol the lines stood out in stark contrast and as in the dirt they faded after a while but I kept working.

A breeze started up as I worked. I was concentrating so hard to get all the lines right I did not notice it at first, but as it got stronger I could smell the dragon's breath and realized he was coming. It was no breeze, but the draft of the dragon's wings. I kept carving while he flew closer.

The tree began to sway from his powerful flapping wings. I had to grab the trunk to keep from falling off, but I kept carving. I had three lines left. The tree swayed so hard it made my stomach turn. I grimaced and closed my eyes, gripping the tree hard. The dragon flew past the tree and landed in front of his cave. I drew another line.

The tree swayed again. I fought against the urge to vomit. My stomach felt as though it was rolling around inside of me. As the tree bent back and stood still for a moment I drew another line. I was flung forward again. I held on tight and looked behind me. The dragon was stomping toward me, his chest growing as he took in a large breath. The tree paused in its violent swaying. I drew the last line. The symbol lit up, every line began to glow with a blinding red light. The tree took me for another ride, paused, and then started bringing me toward the mountain again. I let go.

My body flew toward the mountain, thrown from its branches like a stone shot from a sling. I hit the thick bushes and felt the wind go out of my lungs. I pulled my arms up to my face to block the fierce heat of the dragon's immense blast of fire as it devoured the tree. The heat was painful. I thought for sure that I was being burned alive though the flames did not touch me. I was working to catch my breath when I saw the flames being engulfed by the majestic red cold of the magic.

It looked like a giant tree carved out of brilliant ruby shining against the now drab maroon sky. I tried to stand but my legs gave out from under me. They hurt but I did not think they were broken. I stood up, clutching the talon, and forced my legs to carry me off the mountain. Everything around me had been red this whole time but now the enormous tree was causing the rest of the world to disappear into its ever reaching crimson branches.

I stumbled forward, tripping on a rock and falling into the portal. The cold enveloped me. My legs stopped hurting and I could not feel anything anymore.

The cold expelled me from its bright glow. I fell onto the gloriously brown dirt. I looked up and saw the green trees. I had never loved the color green so much. Past their wonderfully dull branches the sky was a pale blue.

Then I heard my horse blow air through his lips as if to say, "Hey look at me! I am more interesting than those trees up there!"

Fristle had not left. I was so happy to see him. I got up and hobbled over to my horse with the red talon in hand and hugged his neck. Somehow I made it in the saddle. I rode home for the last time as a prince to become a royal wizard for ages to come.

ABOUT THE AUTHOR

Dan first started writing stories in elementary school, where he and a friend would skip lunch and recess once a month to eat in the library while hearing all about the new books on the shelves. His love for reading, as with visual art and music, has now extended into creating his own fiction. He is also a huge fan of podcasting, and all of his stories are available for free in audio. He works as a digital artist and lives in Washington State with his beautiful family of seven.

Thank you for reading my story! For more about me check out my website where I blog about my writing journey, write and podcast book reviews, and have links to many more free stories both in eBook and audio book formats: www.DanDanTheArtMan.com